P9-DVM-769

Space Shuttle Blasts Off!

Peter Bently
Illustrated by Louise Conway

Space Shuttle is on the launch pad at the Space Center.

The tank and rocket boosters are full of fuel.

"We're going to collect a **broken satellite,"** says Commander Mandy.

When the **astronauts** are strapped in, the ground crew locks the shuttle door. In the control room, the **countdown** begins.

The astronauts do their last checks. Everything is working fine.

"All systems go!" says Commander Mandy. "Prepare for lift-off!"

Ten-nine-eight . . .

Commander Mandy starts the main engines.

Seven-six-five-four . . .

"Maximum power!" shouts Commander Mandy.

Three-two-one . . .

Whoosh!

"Lift off!"

With a terrific **blast**, Space Shuttle **rises** from the launch pad.

Space Shuttle soars **higher** and **higher**.
Soon it is high above the **ocean**.

"Release the rocket boosters!"
shouts Commander Mandy.

"Check!" says Copilot Andy, flipping a switch.

The empty **rocket boosters** fall away.

They **splash** down into the sea.

A **ship** is waiting to collect them.

The crew can see **Earth** below as Space Shuttle **flies** into **space**.

"Release the fuel tank!" orders Commander Mandy.

Clunk!

"Check!" says Copilot Andy.

The empty fuel tank **burns up** as it **tumbles** back to Earth.

Commander Mandy **steers** Space Shuttle into **orbit** around Earth.

"Look, that must be the **broken satellite!**" says Copilot Andy.

Space Shuttle **moves** into position below the satellite. Commander Mandy **opens** the **cargo doors**.

Copilot Andy moves a **joystick** to control the **robot arm**.

Whirr!

"Easy does it," says Commander Mandy.

The arm grips the **satellite** and pulls it into the **cargo bay**.

"What a **weird satellite!**" says Commander Mandy.

The crew prepare to close the cargo doors.
Suddenly, they hear a strange sound.

Knock! Knock!

“Maybe the cargo doors are stuck,” says Commander Mandy. “I’ll go outside and look. It’s spacewalk time!”

Commander Mandy puts on her **space suit** and **helmet.** The shuttle door opens and she floats out into space.

She comes face to face with—an alien!

"You've got my spaceship!" says the alien.

"Let us go or my children will be late for school on Mars!"

"Whoops, sorry!" says Commander Mandy. "We thought you were a satellite!"

Space Shuttle releases the alien spaceship.
"Thanks Earthlings," says the alien.
"Next stop Mars!"

Zooom!

The spaceship
flies off.

The astronauts soon spot the **real** broken **satellite**. They load it into the cargo bay . . .

. . . and close the **cargo doors**. **Click!**

"Mission accomplished!" says Commander Mandy.

Space Shuttle glides back down to Earth. It **lands** with a gentle **bump** and rolls to a halt.

The **crew transporter** collects the crew.

Hold on—**Who is that?**

It's a stowaway
alien!

"Space Shuttle is
more fun than school!"
she squeaks.

"Uh-oh!" sighs
Commander Mandy.

"Space Shuttle to
blast off again!"

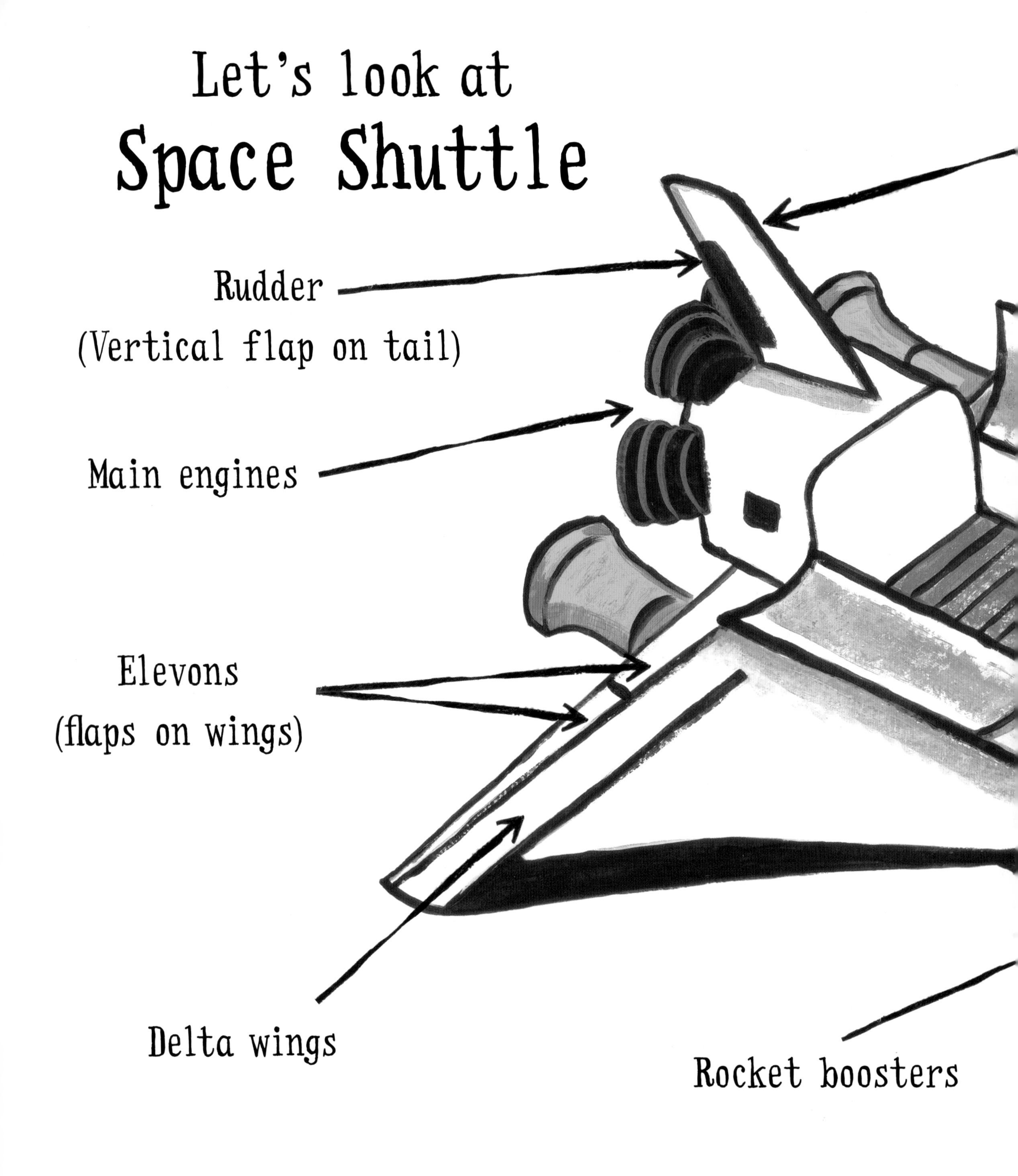
Let's look at
Space Shuttle
Rudder
(Vertical flap on tail)
Main engines
Elevons
(flaps on wings)
Delta wings
Rocket boosters

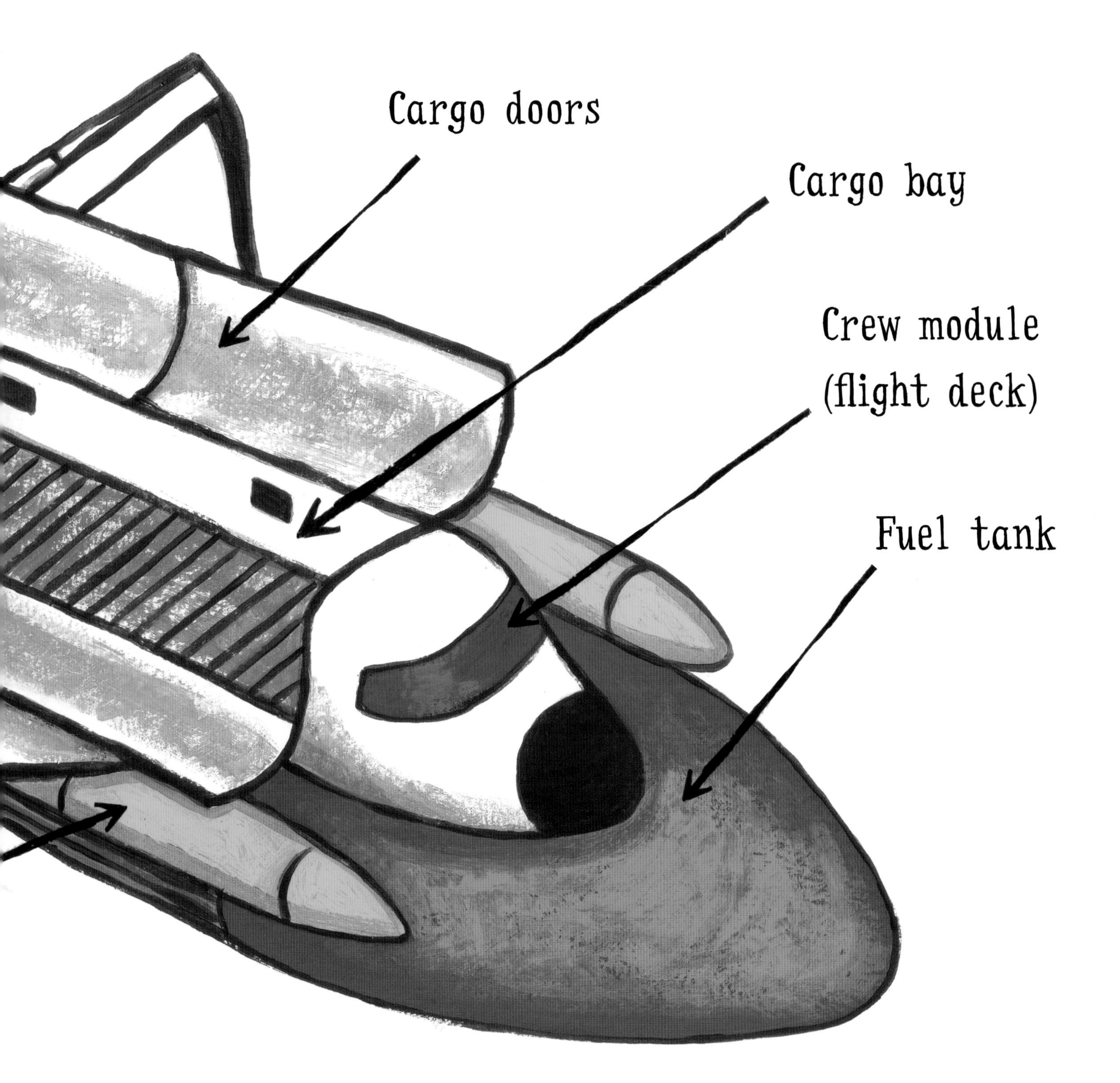
Vertical stabilizer (tail)
Cargo doors
Cargo bay
Crew module
(flight deck)
Fuel tank

Other Space Vehicles

Shuttle Carrier Aircraft

Crawler-transporter

Fuel tank transporter

Crew transporter

For Clyst St. Mary
Primary School, Devon P.B.

For Gavin—your support
means the world L.C.

Designer: Verity Clark
Art Director: Laura Roberts-Jensen
Editors: Tasha Percy and Sophie Hallam
Editorial Director: Victoria Garrard

First published in the United States by
QEB Publishing, Inc.
3 Wrigley, Suite A
Irvine, CA 92618

www.qed-publishing.co.uk

A CIP record for this book is available from the Library of Congress.

ISBN 978 1 60992 792 9
Printed in China